LITTLE BRAVE
A TRADITIONAL SIOUX FOLKTALE

adapted by Emily Kavicky
illustrated by Cheryl Kirk Noll

Harcourt
SCHOOL PUBLISHERS

Printed in China

ISBN 10: 0-15-350980-5
ISBN 13: 978-0-15-350980-3

Ordering Options
ISBN 10: 0-15-350601-6 (Grade 4 On-Level Collection)
ISBN 13: 978-0-15-350601-7 (Grade 4 On-Level Collection)
ISBN 10: 0-15-357933-1 (package of 5)
ISBN 13: 978-0-15-357933-2 (package of 5)

D0464397

2 3 4 5 6 7 8 9 10 985 12 11 10 09 08 07

Many years ago, a whole village moved away from its winter camp to a place that had warmer weather. The people of the village pitched their tents on the edge of a forest. Every night, the elders told stories of the magnificent animals that lived in the forest. They also warned the people to be careful for there were wolves and bears in the forest.

There were children in the village who had never seen a wolf or a bear. One day, the children decided to go into the forest to look for these animals. They asked a playmate named Brave to go along with them.

Brave was a playful fellow who took enormous pleasure in playing tricks on people. Earlier that afternoon, Brave decided to play a trick on his little sister, White Feather. He hid behind the tent, and when White Feather walked by, he jumped out and yelled, "BOO!" Poor little White Feather ran to her mother, crying. Brave's mother, Wenona, saw the girl crying, and she became very distressed.

"Someday you will go too far, Brave, because it is not right to scare people and play tricks on them," Wenona scolded. As Brave walked through the camp, he heard his playmates calling to him.

"Let's go into the forest to find bears and wolves," they said.

"Aren't you afraid?" wondered Brave.

"Of course not!" declared Silver Cloud.

"Why should we be afraid? Wolves and bears are just silly animals," insisted Running Deer.

Just then, Brave had a fabulous idea. "Of course I will go with you, but I must finish my chores first. I will meet you in the forest where the great oak stands."

The rest of the children went off into the forest by the great oak tree and waited and waited. "Where is Brave?" wondered Running Deer.

Meanwhile, Brave had crept into the chief's
tent and found a mask made of feathers, fur, and
animal teeth. Chief Motega used the mask during
ceremonies around the campfire. Brave put on the
mask and went off into the forest.

Back at the oak tree, the children heard strange
sounds coming from the forest. They began to feel
afraid. Suddenly, a frightful animal appeared! It was
Brave, wearing the scary mask and growling like a
wolf. The children screamed and ran out of the
forest. Running behind them was Brave, waving his
arms wildly and making growling sounds.

The children ran screaming into the center of the camp and headed for their tents. The tents of the village all stood in a circle, facing one another. The mothers of the children ran to see what was the matter.

Just then, Brave came running into the village, still wearing the mask. "It's me, Little Brave!" he shouted.

The women, seeing such a fright, yelled and began to run. Brave ran to his mother's tent, scaring her and White Feather terribly. Wenona and White Feather ran away, knocking over the kettle that held dinner. There was complete confusion in the village, with people running everywhere.

Finally, Brave took off the mask. "It's me, Little Brave!" he exclaimed.

The children and women stopped running, and they all stopped to stare at Brave. By that time, the men had heard the yelling from the forest, and they had rushed back from their hunting to see what was the matter.

Chief Motega stepped forward and boomed, "Little Brave, this time you have gone too far! You must learn to show respect for people."

Little Brave's mother declared, "Little Brave, this is absolutely the last time you will scare people!"

Slowly, the people in the village returned to their
tents where pots and kettles had been spilled when
they ran away. Wenona cleaned up the soup that
had spilled from the kettle.

That night, at the campfire, Nashota, the
medicine woman, told stories. The people danced
around the fire, shaking rattles and playing drums.
Brave sat alone at the edge of the campfire. Before
long, Silver Cloud came by, and Little Brave gloated,
"I thought you weren't afraid of bears or wolves."

"Little Brave," said Silver Cloud, "you are the
only one who thinks your tricks are the least bit
funny." With that, she stomped away.

The next day, the people of the village went about their tasks. The women gathered nuts and berries and ground them into meal for supper. The men went out to hunt, joined by some of the older boys. The children did their chores, and when they were finished, they played games with hoops.

No one spoke to Brave. When he went to visit his playmates, they told him they were busy with chores. The women of the village grabbed their kettles out of his way when he walked by. The men and older boys did not ask him to join them.

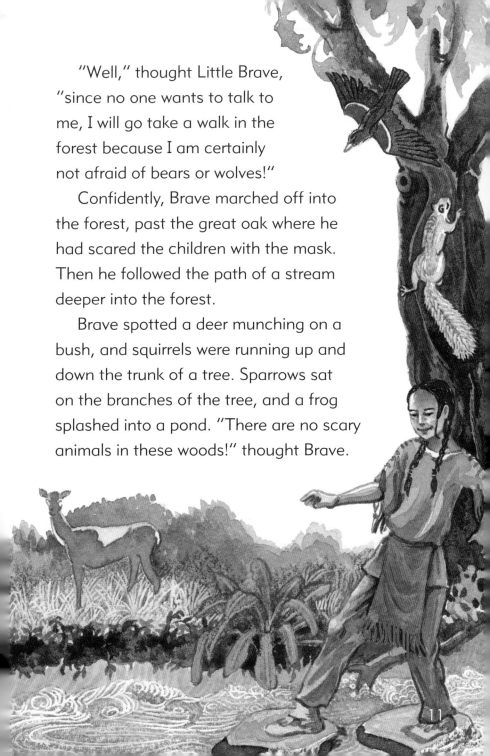

"Well," thought Little Brave, "since no one wants to talk to me, I will go take a walk in the forest because I am certainly not afraid of bears or wolves!"

Confidently, Brave marched off into the forest, past the great oak where he had scared the children with the mask. Then he followed the path of a stream deeper into the forest.

Brave spotted a deer munching on a bush, and squirrels were running up and down the trunk of a tree. Sparrows sat on the branches of the tree, and a frog splashed into a pond. "There are no scary animals in these woods!" thought Brave.

Just then, through the bushes, Brave saw the face of an animal he had never seen before. The animal looked fierce with its large, round eyes, very sharp teeth, and two pointy ears. Brave began to run, very frightened. "It must be a wolf," Brave thought.

As he ran, Brave caught his foot in the roots of a tree. He fell, landing on the ground. He could not free his foot from the tangled roots. "Oh, no," he thought. "If I cannot get free, the wolf will find me. I must be very quiet!"

Anxiously, Brave freed his foot from the tree roots. Slowly, he crept back to the bush where he had seen the animal's face. To his tremendous surprise, the face behind the bush was nothing but a rock! The way the sun shone through the leaves cast shadows, and the shadows only looked like the face of an animal.

"The sun is playing tricks on my eyes!" thought Brave. Just then, the wind began to whistle, and the noise of the wind sounded like an animal.

"The wind is playing tricks with my ears, too!" thought Brave. Now he knew what it was like to be tricked!

It was getting dark, and the people of the village began to worry about Brave. His playmates missed him. No one could stay angry for long because Brave really was a likable fellow.

Suddenly, Brave appeared from the forest, and he ran to his mother and White Feather. "I am sorry for playing tricks, and I promise it will never happen again," he said as they hugged him.

That night at the campfire, Brave told the people of the village how sorry he was. Chief Motega smiled and patted Brave on the head. "You have learned a great lesson, Little Brave. Now come and join us," said the chief. Brave joined in with the people of the village, and they all danced by the light of the fire.

Think Critically

1. At what point in the story did Brave go too far?

2. Brave's mother, Wenona, is distressed when White Feather cries. What is a word that means the same as *distressed* on page 4?

3. How did Little Brave gain the respect of the village?

4. Do you think the children like Little Brave? Explain why or why not.

5. Do you think it is okay to play tricks on people? Explain your answer.

 Social Studies

Make a Mask Many Native American tribes used masks in their tribal ceremonies. Find pictures of Native American masks in a book. Then draw a picture of a mask you might wear around a campfire at night.

School-Home Connection Discuss this story with a family member. Then talk about how things will get better for Little Brave after he is sorry for playing tricks.

Word Count: 1,247